FIND FERGUS

The List of things to Find

1. Fergus
(a bear who looks like this)

2. Just Fergus

To my wonderful agent, Jennifer.
Thank you for finding a home for Fergus
and all the other stories I do.

All rights reserved. Published in the United States by Doubleday, an imprint of Random House Children's Books,
a division of Penguin Random House LLC, New York.

Doubleday and the colophon are registered trademarks of Penguin Random House LLC.

Visit us on the Web! rhcbooks.com

Educators and librarians, for a variety of teaching tools, visit us at RHTeachersLibrarians.com

Library of Congress Cataloging-in-Publication Data
Name: Boldt, Mike, author, illustrator.
Title: Find Fergus / by Mike Boldt.
Description: First edition. | New York : Doubleday Books for Young Readers, [2020] | Audience: Ages 3–7. |
Summary: Fergus the bear wants to play hide-and-seek with the reader, but will need help—and practice—to hide well.
Identifiers: LCCN 2019050656 (print) | LCCN 2019050657 (ebook)
ISBN 978-1-9848-4902-1 (hardback) | ISBN 978-1-9848-4903-8 (library binding) | ISBN 978-1-9848-4904-5 (ebook)
Subjects: CYAC: Hide-and-seek—Fiction. | Bears—Fiction.
Classification: LCC PZ7.B635863 Fin 2020 (print) | LCC PZ7.B635863 (ebook) | DDC [E]—dc23

ISBN 978-0-593-38018-5 (proprietary edition)

MANUFACTURED IN CHINA
10 9 8 7 6 5 4 3

This Imagination Library edition is published by Random House Children's Books, a division of
Penguin Random House, exclusively for Dolly Parton's Imagination Library, a not-for-profit program
designed to inspire a love of reading and learning, sponsored in part by The Dollywood Foundation.
Penguin Random House's trade editions of this work are available wherever books are sold.

Let's go

FIND FERGUS

He's hiding on the next page!

(by MIKE BOLDT)

Doubleday Books for Young Readers

Fergus!

We already found you!

That was too easy.

Try hiding again.

That was easy as well.
Is there something
you can hide behind?

Oh, Fergus.

You're not very good at this.

But that's okay!

We're going to help you.

Start by hiding in a crowd.

A crowd is more

than three, Fergus.

That's definitely a crowd!
Okay. Now think **bigger.**

Too big!

That's the right size . . .
but you're **not** a moose.

Still not a moose, Fergus.

Try bears.

How about

NOT polar bears.

One Minute, Please

I see you're not quite ready.
We'll do a countdown while
you find a great spot to hide.

Oh, WOW!

Way to go, Fergus!

Fergus, that's much better!
Wait, you're not done yet?
Okay, we'll find you.
ONE.
    LAST.
        TIME.

10, 9, 8, 7, 6, 5, 4, 3, 2, 1 . . .

Ready or not, here we come!

FERGUS!!!

Errr . . . Fergus? Where are you?

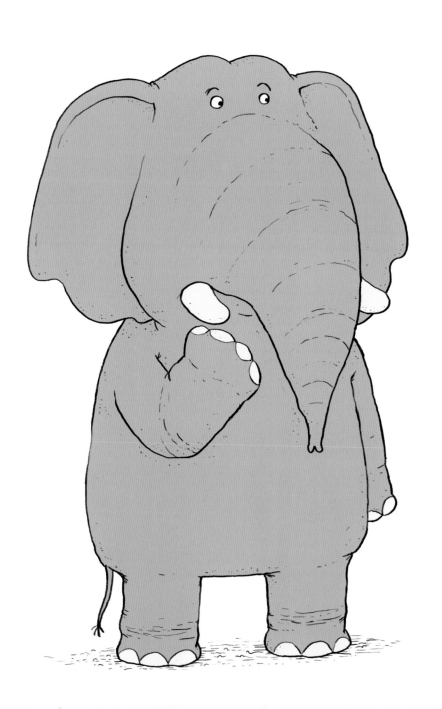

See, Fergus, you just
needed a little practice.
Now you're great at hiding!
Ummm, Fergus . . .
where are you going
with that marker?

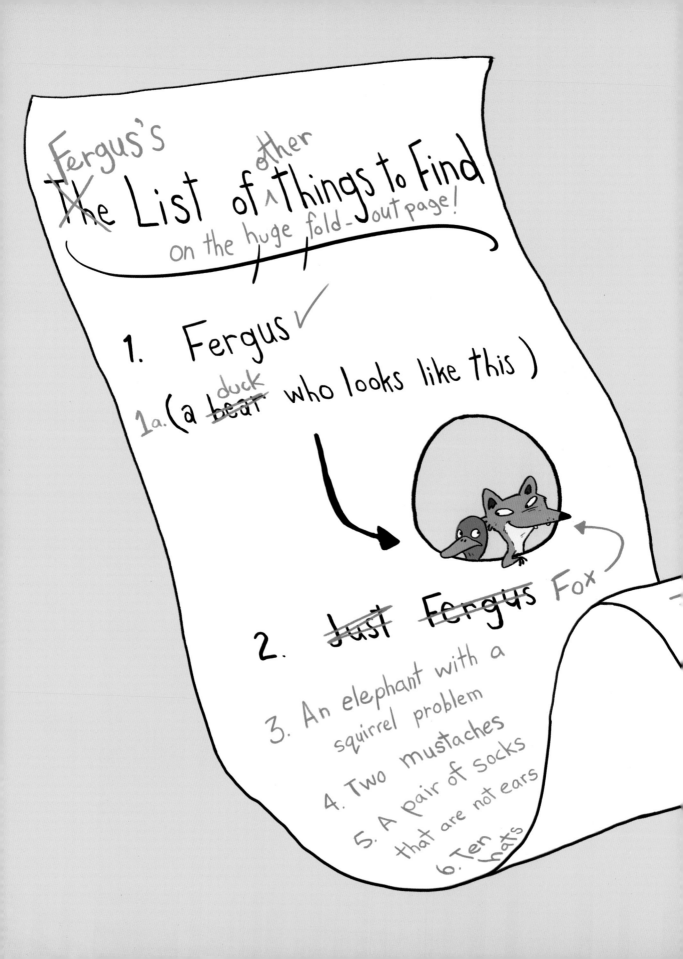

ur neckties

Squirrel carrying a rabbit

ho is carrying another rabbit

Glasses worn on the wrong end

0. A moose with pretend antlers

11. Seven animals with carrots

12. Two who are too cool

13. A seriously stinky situation

14. An animal who knows the time